Smile with Simon

Written By:

Patricia Ann Simon R.N.

Author of Simon and the Buddy Branch

Illustrated By:

Valerie McCord

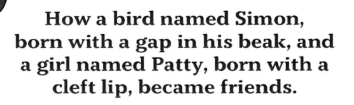

How a bird named Simon,
born with a gap in his beak, and
a girl named Patty, born with a
cleft lip, became friends.

ISBN: 978-0-9988786-0-7 (sc)
ISBN: 978-0-9988786-1-4 (e)

Library of Congress Control Number: 2017905908

I would like to thank my family. They helped shape my personality, face obstacles, and share credit on every goal I have achieved. They taught me about kindness, and that everyone is different and beautiful.

I would also like to thank my wife, Colleen Fallon, for her constant love and support. I love her with every beat of my heart.

And finally, to my wonderful friends. You saw beyond my scar. You gave me unconditional love and have made my heart smile.

FOREWORD

Writing a book addressed to very young children requires special skills and talent.

Writing a children's book for children born with facial differences, based on personal experience, requires not only skills and talent, but also courage.

Patricia Simon was able to write two colorful books, *Smile with Simon* and *Simon and the Buddy Branch,* in an effort to educate children, parents, and educators dealing with children born with facial differences.

The message is simple but also very powerful: be tolerant and embrace children born with facial differences. Be supportive because they are wonderful human beings and deserve warm acceptance, not exclusion.

There is a message for the children born with facial differences as well: be brave—you are great kids, and with the support of your doctors, family, and community, you will have a successful future.

I spent my entire career treating patients born with facial differences, and I want to congratulate Patricia Simon for this beautiful initiative.

As a patient of mine said once, "It does not matter how you look outside but how you feel inside!"

This patient, Natalie, is about to graduate from college and enter the workforce with a big smile.

Thanks, Patricia!

Mimis Cohen MD, FACS, FAAP
Professor and Chief Division of
Plastic, Reconstruction and Cosmetic Surgery
University of Illinois, Chicago
Director Craniofacial Center UIC

Once upon a time,
there lived a **bright red cardinal
named Simon.**

Simon's favorite thing to do was
to fly from tree to tree,
chirping as loudly as he could.

Simon was not an ordinary bird.
He had a scar in the middle of his beak.

Simon's family and friends called his scar his
"badge of courage."
This is the story of how he earned it.

Simon hatched from his shell
with baby-brown feathers
and a gap in his beak.

The gap made it hard for him
to eat and grow strong enough to fly.

Simon's mother and father
loved him very much, and wanted to help.

But Simon was smaller
and weaker than his
brothers and sisters.

One day, Simon was chirping his favorite song and accidentally fell out of the nest.

"Help!" he cried as he tumbled to the ground.

Luckily, Simon landed on a soft patch of grass.
"Are you okay?" his mother asked.

"I'm okay, Mom!" Simon replied,
"But I can't fly back to the nest!"

Simon's mother knew she needed to find
help fast. "I know just who to ask," she said.

Chirping loudly and flying as fast as she could,
Simon's mother headed straight to the Garcias' backyard.

The Garcias had a bird feeder set up in front
of a big window. Their daughter Patty loved to
sit by the window and watch the birds.

"Help!" Simon's mother flew to the glass when she saw
Patty at the window. **"Simon needs help,"**
she chirped while fluttering her wings.

As soon as Patty saw Simon's mother, she knew something was wrong.
Patty ran and got her mom, Mrs. Garcia, and they came outside.

"There!" Patty pointed
to Simon's mom.
**"I wonder what
she wants,"**
said Patty's mom.

"Follow me!"
Simon's mother tweeted.

Patty and her mother followed Simon's mom to where
Simon was sitting on the grass.

**"Look mom,
it's a baby bird!"**
said Patty.

Patty's mom said,
"Do you see his beak,
Patty?"

When Patty saw the gap in Simon's beak, tears filled her eyes. **"He's just like me, Mom."** She pointed to the scar on her lip.

"Can we help him?" Patty asked.
"We can try, honey," Patty's mom said.
"We can try."

Patty's mom hurried back to the house and
returned with a shoebox and a soft towel.

Gently, she picked Simon up and
put him in the box.

"Let's go see Dr. Cruz,"
Patty's mom said.

Patty and her mom took Simon to see their veterinarian, Dr. Cruz.

"Oh my," Dr. Cruz said when she saw Simon's beak, "this is unusual."

"His beak has a gap like my lip used to have," Patty said. **"Can you help him?"**

"I'll try my very best," Dr. Cruz answered. "Do you have a name for your little friend?"

"Simon." Patty smiled. "His name is Simon."

While Patty and her mother waited for Dr. Cruz to fix Simon's beak, they talked about the scar on Patty's lip.

"You were very small when the doctors fixed your cleft lip," Patty's mom said.

"Will Simon have a scar too?" Patty asked.

"Yes, but it will be easier for him to eat and sing."

"Sometimes kids laugh at my scar," said Patty. "Do you think other birds will make fun of Simon?"

"I don't know, but I hope not," Patty's mom said. **"Do you remember what we called your scar?"**

"My badge of courage." Patty smiled and touched her lip. "Now Simon will have a badge of courage too!"

When Simon woke up after his operation, he saw
Dr. Cruz, Patty, and her mom looking down at him.

"Eeep!" he chirped. His head was fuzzy and his beak felt heavy.
"He's awake..." Patty whispered, tugging on her mother's arm.

"The operation went very well," said Dr. Cruz.
"Simon will be sleepy for a little while,
**but he should be able to eat, drink,
and sing much better now."**

Patty and her mom took Simon home
and gently placed him back in his nest.

"Goodbye, Simon," Patty said. "I'll see you in a couple of days."
Simon's parents were very happy to see him.
They chirped and sang to welcome him home.

The next morning, Simon woke up very hungry. He chirped and chirped until his mother asked, **"Are you hungry? Would you like breakfast?"**

"Oh yes!" Simon opened his beak so his mother could feed him. **He ate and ate until his tummy was full!**

Over the next few days, Simon grew **stronger and stronger.**

He was excited to show his new beak to the other birds, but was also a little scared.

"You have a funny scar on your beak, **but I think you look cool,"** Simon's sister Susie said.

"Simon, you are beautiful inside and out," said Simon's parents.

Soon, all the birds in the neighborhood stopped by to hear Simon's story and admire his new beak.

"The scar on my beak is called a badge of courage," Simon explained. "The nice people in the house next door helped me."

"Well, you look a little different now,"
said Jose, the big black crow, "but that's okay.

**Everyone is different,
but we are all still alike."**